DOLLHOUSE

JC BRATTON

BLUE MILK Publishing

Dollhouse

By JC Bratton

ISBN-13: 978-0-9986453-6-0 (paperback)

ISBN-13: 978-0-9986453-7-7 (e-book)

Library of Congress Control Number: 2020920984

First printing edition, October 2020

Second printing edition, November 2022

Blue Milk Publishing: San Jose, California

PROLOGUE

"THIS HAS GOT to be the greatest thing ever!" John channeled his inner geek as he took his big-ticket item out of its box.

"Aren't you a little old to be playing with *dolls*?" John's wife, Myra, didn't approve of his whimsical purchase.

"Come on, you know I love collecting." John brushed off Myra's comment. "From what the seller told me, this dollhouse was handcrafted in Japan back in the 1930s. Look at the architecture and exquisite detail. It's amazing. It comes with three dolls, furniture, lighting — the whole nine yards."

As John unwrapped the items from their packaging, Myra accidentally bumped into the shipping box and knocked it off the table. Something fell out of the box and slid across the floor.

"Hey, what's this?" Myra asked curiously. She brushed off the packing foam to reveal a book. It was hardcover, brown in color and looked quite old and worn.

John took the book from Myra. He quickly thumbed through the pages.

"It is handwritten, and the penmanship is beautiful — calligraphy. There are three ribbons bookmarking three sections, each one labeled with a name: Muffy, Buffy, and Duffy." John closed the book and then looked back at the dolls in their packaging. "I wonder…"

John unwrapped each doll to uncover that printed on the back label each of the dolls' dresses were their names: Muffy, Buffy, and Duffy.

"Okay, that is a bit creepy," Myra said in a shaky tone.

"Oh, come on; this isn't *Child's Play*. I'm sure it's nothing. In fact, I think it's rather cute; they're probably three sisters." John gave Myra a hug and kissed her forehead. "Just relax and help me move everything over to the den."

———

"I HAVE A BIT OF A HEADACHE," Myra said as she rubbed her temples when entering the den. "The dishes are in the washer now. I think I am going to turn in early tonight. When are you coming to bed?"

John didn't pay attention to Myra; he was too focused on where to place the various pieces of furniture and how to strategically display the dolls.

"Earth to John…" Myra waved her hand across John's face to wake him up from his dollhouse trance.

"Oh, sorry, honey. What did you say?" John looked back at Myra.

"Never mind — just telling you I'm heading to bed," Myra muttered with an annoyed look on her face.

John got up from his chair and gave Myra a kiss.

"Aww, you know you will always be MY doll," John said apologetically.

"Don't stay up too late..." Myra headed upstairs to the bedroom as John sat back down and shifted focus back to his new obsession.

John took each of the dolls and lined them up in a row. There was something mystical about these dolls. Muffy had beautiful, flowing dark hair; Buffy was a natural beauty — she would be a model if she was real; and then there was Duffy — something was off about her. She wasn't as well-kept as the others. She looked a bit mischievous.

"Are you the bastard child, Duffy?" John snorted to himself.

The temperature seemed to drop suddenly after he said those words.

"Shoot, I bet I left the kitchen window open."

John walked into the kitchen and discovered that the window was, in fact, open, and it began to drizzle. There was a bottle of wine on the kitchen counter, so John decided to pour a glass and take a sip — or two, or three. After finishing the bottle, he proceeded to close the window; however, when looking outside, he could have sworn he saw someone — a woman wearing all white. John rubbed his eyes and looked out the window again; there was no one there.

"Okay, John, you had enough wine," he told himself.

When he got back to the den, he found the book that came with the dollhouse resting on his chair.

"Wait, how did the book land on my chair? Myra?" John questioned as he looked around the room.

Not one to be frightened easily, he picked it up from his chair, sat down and opened the book to the first page, which contained a string of Japanese characters.

花子さんの所有物

"Okay, not sure what that means," John whispered to himself. The rest of the book was in English, so he dived into the first section: *Muffy...*

PART ONE
MUFFY

"I NEVER SAID THAT. Why do you keep making up stories?" Steve and Monica were at each other's throats constantly. Monica would call Steve a narcissist while Steve would complain that Monica was too sensitive. The two could go back and forth all night, especially when Steve had been drinking heavily.

They had two children: Ken, age seventeen, and Penny, age six. Penny was a complete angel in Ken's eyes: she had long, dark hair that was very soft to the touch. She was very kind and innocent. As Penny's big brother, Ken did his best to shield her from the Mom and Dad drama show.

"Daddy seems to hate Mommy," Penny said as she crawled under her covers.

"Hate is a strong word," Ken said to downplay the situation. "Sometimes grown-ups have disagreements. Don't be scared. Actually, I have something that will cheer you up..."

Ken opened up his backpack to reveal a beautiful doll with dark hair in an "okappa" style. She was wearing a Japanese kimono.

"Her name is Muffy. I bought her at a yard sale."

"I LOVE her!" Penny grabbed Muffy from Ken's hand and started to squeeze the doll very tightly.

"I knew you would like her." Seeing Penny smile was all Ken wanted.

"From what I understand, she was custom made by a brilliant Japanese artist. She put so much passion into her work. And it shows..."

"Muffy, you are going to be my best friend," Penny said as she looked Muffy in the eyes.

"Okay, I'll leave you to get to know your new best friend. I love you, kiddo." Ken kissed his sister good night.

"You are the best brother in the whole world!"

OVER THE NEXT MONTH, Penny and Muffy were inseparable. Penny would bring Muffy to school, have Muffy with her when she ate dinner, and would sleep with Muffy every night. Her parents were too wrapped up in their own perils to notice the profound change in Penny. She had a special friend that wouldn't judge her, that would always be there for her — someone she could take care of. Ken planned to go to college out of state next year, so knowing Penny had something to make her happy was all he could ask for... until Penny got sick.

Over the winter, Penny became very ill. The doctors did not understand what was wrong with her. Some sort of viral infection, maybe? She was in bed for weeks with Muffy by her side. One night, Penny became violently ill and started coughing up blood. She had to be taken to the hospital. When she got there, she awoke briefly only to find that Muffy was not there. With the chaos of trying to get Penny to the hospital, her parents forgot to bring Muffy.

"I need Muffy." Penny fought so hard to speak out loud.

"I'll bring her over; don't worry, kiddo," Ken assured Penny.

When Ken came back with Muffy, he was told that Penny had passed away.

Ken was in so much pain; he lost Penny, the sweet, innocent girl with beautiful long hair — the light of Ken's life. He sat in the hospital chapel and brought Muffy with him.

"Why did you have to take her from me?" Ken looked up and asked God.

Tears rolled down Ken's cheeks. He closed his eyes and just sat quietly. After about thirty minutes, he figured he should join the rest of the family. He grabbed his backpack and went to pick up Muffy — but she wasn't there.

"Wait, where's Muffy?" Ken pondered as he looked all over the chapel.

Steve and Monica found Ken in the chapel to let him know they were going to head back to the house.

"Have you seen Muffy?" Ken asked his parents.

"Muffy?" Steve questioned.

"Yes ... Penny's doll..." Ken said.

"No, I'm afraid we haven't," Monica interjected. "Come on, Ken, let's go home and get some rest."

"Okay, well, let me look around some more, and I'll join you in a bit."

Ken asked the nurses, staff — anyone who could have possibly seen Muffy. No one had seen her.

"I *know* the doll was with me," Ken explained to the head nurse. "She was so important to Penny."

"We'll keep a lookout, Ken," said the RN in charge. "We'll call you right away when we find it. We know it's a difficult time for you and your family. Get some rest. If the doll is here, we'll find it and keep it safe."

EXHAUSTED, Ken made it back to the house. His parents weren't home yet, which was a bit odd. He knew it would be painful, but the first room he needed to enter was Penny's room. The door was closed. Ken opened it and turned on the light to find Muffy in Penny's bed!

Suddenly, Muffy turned her head and looked straight at Ken. Her hair began to grow long like Penny's — right in front of Ken's eyes.

Ken was frozen; in shock.

"Will you be my new best friend?"

PART TWO
BUFFY

"YOU WILL *LOVE* THIS PLACE!" Mike and Amber's real estate agent, Kim Vu, gloated as she let them into the building. "It just came on the market. It's perfect for a professional young couple and probably the best condo you can find near Union Square."

Amber always wanted to live in San Francisco. Growing up in a conservative small town in Texas, she embraced the thought of being in a progressive city that was more in-line with her values. Mike, on the other hand, was born and raised in San Francisco. He had also lived in Tokyo for five years. He would have preferred it if Amber wanted to live in the countryside, like Napa wine country — something a bit slower-paced. But, he was too crazy about Amber to say no. They weren't married yet, and this would be their first time officially living together. When she passed, Mike's grandmother had left him with money for purchasing a home. This new place would be around the corner from his office, so he really couldn't complain.

The unit was on the top floor. The elevator opened, and Kim walked the couple to the condo's entrance.

"Oh my God, it's gorgeous! So much prettier than the photos!" Amber was immediately drawn to the formal entry, French windows, hardwood floors, and vaulted ceiling.

"The kitchen is modern with stainless appliances, gas range, and dishwasher," Kim said as she guided the couple. "There is a circular private bedroom with a walk-in closet. The bathroom was updated last year, and this unit has a washer and dryer. I know not having that was one of the deal-breakers for you, Amber."

Amber was a bit of a "neat freak" and minimalist. Mike, on the other hand, never threw anything away.

"Hey, honey, check this out." Amber pointed out a secret curved closet with built-in shelves.

"Wow! What's this? A secret room?" Mike asked Kim.

"Kinda interesting, huh?" Kim responded. "The previous owner had this made. No particular explanation why, but it's definitely unusual."

Amber looked inside the closet and noticed a doll sitting on the top shelf, dressed in a kimono. It was very beautiful with a warm smile. There was something peculiar about the doll, though. She couldn't quite put her finger on it.

"Oh, don't worry about all the clutter," Kim said as she woke Amber from her trace. "The previous owner plans to have everything cleared out."

"Well, I am definitely excited about this place," Amber said as she held onto Mike. "What do you think, honey?"

Mike was lukewarm, but seeing the happiness on Amber's face, Mike didn't want to disappoint.

"Well, if this place makes you happy, let's seriously consider it," Mike said with a smile and kissed Amber.

"ON MOVE-IN WEEK? SERIOUSLY?" Amber was so frustrated when Mike called her with the news.

"I'm sorry, baby," Mike said apologetically. "There is an emergency with a client in LA, and I need to fly out tonight. I'll be back on Monday."

The new condo was stacked with Mike's boxes. Mike finally promised to pare down on items after the couple watched a few episodes of *Hoarders*. However, much of what had to be unpacked belonged to Mike.

"Well, I am going to start organizing; I get the secret closet." Amber smirked as she tried to get over her disappointment.

"Of course! It's all yours. I'll call you when I get to LA." As Mike hung up on Amber, he couldn't help but to feel a bit unsettled. The natural protector in Mike was not happy that Amber would be by herself the first night at the new place.

ABOUT FIVE HOURS had passed and Amber was able to get a lot done. The secret closet was almost to Amber's satisfaction; she was able to fill it with her ceramic cats, snow globes, travel items... After looking at the full closet, Amber mused to herself, "Wait, who is the real pack rat?"

As she unpacked the last box for the closet, the doorbell rang. Amber opened the door to find no one on the other side, except for a small box.

"Ugh, I'll bet it's one of Mike's boxes; must have left it downstairs," Amber thought aloud as she picked up the box and opened it.

"Oh my God!" To Amber's shock, the package contained a

doll — the same doll that she had seen in the secret closet! In addition to the doll was a sealed envelope.

"What is all of this?"

Amber placed the doll on the kitchen counter and opened the envelope. There was a note with pasted letters and words from magazine clippings. The message was very clear:

If I cannot have you, no one can.

In addition to the letter was a photo of Mike and Amber, with Amber's face scratched out violently in red ink. Amber screamed in terror! She dropped the photo and ran to her phone to call Mike.

"Hello, you've reached Mike. I'm not able to come to the phone right now. Leave your name and number, and I'll get back with you as soon as I can."

"Mike, I need to talk to you; call me back as soon as possible."

Amber sent a text as well.

"Come on, Mike! Where are you?" Amber then looked at the clock; it was 7 PM. "Shoot, he's probably on the plane; he won't have access to calls or texts for about an hour."

Who would play such a sick joke? And why the doll? Amber looked back to the kitchen, and the doll was missing! Suddenly, chills travelled across Amber's body. She knew she wasn't alone.

"Amber..." It was a soft female voice, and it started giggling. "Come and find me!"

There was only one place she could be, Amber thought — the secret closet.

———

"AMBER!" Mike shouted as he rushed into the condo. He took the first flight back from LA, as Amber was not returning his calls.

"Mike?" a soft voice said. "Come and find me."

"Amber?" Mike said hesitantly. The secret closet light was illuminated, and the voice sounded as if it was coming from there. Mike opened the closet to find a young, beautiful Japanese woman with dark hair and pale skin.

"Buffy!" Mike shouted in terror. "But...you're dead! You killed yourself the night we broke up."

"Shhhh...It doesn't matter anymore. We will be together forever."

"No!" Mike screamed.

Behind Buffy was a new doll on the toy shelf — it was Amber, dressed in a kimono.

PART THREE
DUFFY

"HEY, Pam, thanks for taking us in," Sam said while giving her a hug.

"Of course; you and Kimmie are welcome to stay as long as you want — this is your house, too," assured Pam.

"Thanks, but I don't hope to inconvenience you more than six months. Just need to get the insurance settled and the house repaired."

There had been a really bad storm. Sam's wife, Jill, was on her way home after a late shift at the hospital. Lightning struck a tree branch, and it fell on the driver's side of Jill's car, killing her instantly. Sam and Kimmie did not learn of Jill's death until the next morning, as the storm also produced a nocturnal tornado. Sam and Kimmie were able to stay safe in the storm cellar, but the house was badly damaged.

Sam had no family in the area. The only nearby relatives were Jill's. Pam was Jill's aunt, a widower in her late 60s. She owned a two-story home with three bedrooms, two bathrooms and an attic. Her husband had passed away ten years ago, before Kimmie was born.

At age seven, Kimmie had a general understanding of death. She knew her mom was not coming back. She wasn't exhibiting any noticeable anxieties, but it was too soon to tell.

Kimmie was pretty quiet as she and Sam grabbed their belongings from the car. Pam noticed that Kimmie seemed down, so she thought of a way to cheer her up.

"Kimmie, did you know your mom had a special friend when she was around your age? Her name is Duffy. Want to meet her?"

Kimmie, still somber, nodded in agreement.

"What are you talking about, Pam?" Sam gave a questioning look.

"Didn't Jill ever tell you? When she was around Kimmie's age, she had a dollhouse. It was custom-made in Japan. Jill's father did a lot of traveling for work and picked it up in Osaka. There were at least four dolls at one point with the dollhouse, but over the years things get misplaced, thrown away... Duffy is the only remaining doll."

Pam, Sam, and Kimmie walked upstairs to Kimmie's new bedroom. Pam had anticipated gifting the dollhouse and Duffy to Kimmie, so it was all ready for her arrival.

Pam picked up Duffy and formally introduced her.

"Duffy, meet Kimmie. Kimmie, meet Duffy. I'm sure you'll become great friends."

Duffy was a porcelain doll wearing a kimono. She had some scars on her face, maybe from being played with a lot or just wear and tear over the years. Still, the doll seemed to bring a smile to Kimmie's face.

IT WAS AROUND 3:30 AM, and Kimmie was in bed with Duffy by her side. Kimmie felt something touch her hand. She slowly opened her eyes to see a woman with long, dark hair wearing a white gown. She looked a bit like Jill, but it was hard to tell in the dark. For some reason, Kimmie was not afraid.

"Mommy?" Kimmie asked.

"Shhh," the woman said, holding her index finger to her lips. "Come with me."

While holding onto Duffy, Kimmie followed the woman down the hall and up the stairs to the attic. The attic door was wide open.

Sam couldn't sleep. He watched some old videos of Jill. He missed her terribly. Suddenly, Sam thought he heard footsteps. He went to Kimmie's room to see her door was open, and that she wasn't there.

Worried, Sam shouted her name: "Kimmie!"

A horrific scream came from the attic. Sam raced up to the attic and froze in terror as he saw a girl *inside* a mirror in the attic. She grabbed Kimmie and pulled her into the mirror.

"Daddy!" Kimmie screamed as she tried to escape.

"Kimmie! No!" Sam was unable to move; a force stopped him in his tracks. Kimmie and the girl in the mirror vanished, leaving behind Duffy.

"Sam?" a woman's voice asked.

"Pam — it's Kimmie! She's gone!" Sam was able to move again and rushed over to the mirror.

As Sam looked in the mirror, he noticed that the woman behind him was not Pam. It was a woman with long dark hair and wearing a white gown. She was carrying Duffy.

"Sam, welcome to my dollhouse."

Sam turned around and screamed as he noticed that the person talking was not the woman in white; it was Duffy.

EPILOGUE

"UM, OKAY..." John said to himself in disbelief after he read the last page. "There is no freaking way any of that happened; these are *dolls*. This is a *dollhouse*. *It's not real!*

"Muffy, you are not Penny.

"Buffy, you are not Amber.

"And, Duffy ... well, you already creep me out. But, nah... you are *just a doll*.

"And this is just a dollhouse crafted by some person in Japan. Get a grip, John. Just call up the guy you bought the dollhouse from in the morning and get this whole thing sorted. In the meantime..."

John placed each of the dolls in their rooms. He turned out the lights in the den.

———

"NO FREAKING WAY..." John murmured to himself as he brushed his teeth and got ready for bed. It was 3:33 AM.

John entered the bedroom. It was dark, but the nightlight

was on. Myra appeared to be sound asleep. He crawled under the covers and gently placed his arm around his wife. But, something was wrong. The woman next to him was not Myra. It was the woman in white with Japanese characters written in blood red across her gown:

花子さんの所有物
(Property of Hanako-San)

"Bloody Mary!" John gasped.

ABOUT THE AUTHOR

Growing up loving horror and mystery tales, JC Bratton writes stories that pay homage to the Point Horror novels she would read as a kid: stories such as *Slumber Party* by Christopher Pike and *Twisted* by RL Stine. Some of her biggest influences are Alfred Hitchcock, Lois Duncan, Stephen King, and Richard Matheson.

Although she hopes for that Netflix movie deal, JC still has her day job and lives in the heart of Silicon Valley with her husband, stepsons, and cats.

amazon.com/author/jcbratton

youtube.com/@jcbratton

ABOUT BLUE MILK PUBLISHING

Blue Milk Publishing represents independent authors of both fiction and non-fiction works.

Please visit **bluemilk.co** *for more information.*

Non-Fiction

The Cheating Boyfriend (And Other Organizational Indiscretions) (January 2017) by Jenny Hayes Carhart, MSOD, PHR

Fiction

Who's at the Door? (January 2020) by JC Bratton

Parasomnia (June 2020) by JC Bratton

Dollhouse (October 2020) by JC Bratton

Who's Back at the Door? (October 2023) by JC Bratton

JC Bratton's Things That Go Bump in the Night, Volume One: Urban Legends (October 2023) by JC Bratton

Made in the USA
Middletown, DE
11 June 2024